All About

TRAINING SHAMU

Published by

THIRD STORY BOOKS™

955 Connecticut Avenue, Suite 1302

Bridgeport, Connecticut 06607

ISBN 1-884506-11-9

Distributed to the trade by

Andrews & McMeel

4900 Main Street

Kansas City, Missouri 64112

Library of Congress Catalog Card Number: 93-61830

Printed in Singapore

All About

TRAINING SHAMU

Written by Jane Resnick

FEATURING *Sea World®* PHOTOGRAPHY

THIRD™
STORY
BOOKS

Training animals is not a new idea. It's ancient. How would man have crossed the desert without camels? Today, we still train animals, to live with us and to help us work.

EdUCated animals

By studying whales we learn about their complex lives and how man can take care of them and the environment.

The information about killer whales gathered at SEA WORLD is shared with families through educational programs.

FACT By training and working with whales we learn about their growth, their development and how they raise their young. We gather information that could not be gathered from observations of wild populations.

By training whales, we can educate people about them, develop relationships with them and stimulate them.

shamu,

KILLER
WHALE

Killer whales are mammals. About 55 million years ago their ancestors lived on land. Then they returned to the sea to become mighty ocean predators. These striking black-and-white creatures are found in all the oceans of the world.

Killer whales have front (pectoral) flippers with the same bone structure as land mammals, but modified for the water.
They have a dorsal fin (above left)
and two flukes that form their tails (above right).

Whales breathe through a "blowhole." Swimming below water, this humpback whale holds its breath for up to 10 minutes. Then it begins to exhale when it breaks the surface.

PODS

Killer whales live in "pods," groups of about five to 30 members and, like lions and wolves, hunt cooperatively. Imagine coming face-to-face with a *group* of killer whales!

Shamu and his trainer work on their relationship.

SCH OO L
DAYS

Shamu practices and exercises every day, just like any athlete.

8

At SEA WORLD, every day is a school day for killer whales. Shamu goes to classes all the time. He even has recess. And sometimes it's hard to tell one from the other. In learning sessions, Shamu works on his performance. During exercise sessions, he does laps for fun. At socializing sessions, he joins other whales and their trainers for some splashing around.

SHAMU'S FAVORITE CLASS

All these activities keep Shamu healthy. But the relationship session where Shamu and his trainer spend time together—just the two of them—is a favorite.

Because killer whales are animals that live in groups, they socialize at SEA WORLD.

Shamu is "spyhopping," a behavior that helps him eavesdrop on his surroundings. Many of the behaviors seen at SEA WORLD are those that whales do in the wild.

Learning behavior

Do killer whales learn like we do? While the basic principles of learning are the same, animals only learn in response to their needs. They need to find food, to avoid predators, and to reproduce. Perhaps when animals change their behavior, they are not "thinking" as we do, but they do learn. And Shamu shows us that what they learn can be amazing.

DIFFERENT abilities

It's easy to think that animals feel the way we do. But they don't. As "smart" as Shamu appears, he is a killer whale, and he probably does not have human characteristics or human emotions. So it's best to respect his great ability. And remember that it's different from ours.

"Breaching" is a natural killer whale behavior.

Shamu "learns" through a variety of methods, but he probably doesn't have human emotions.

The young whale follows the leader.

Copycats

Doing what comes naturally is one way that whales learn at SEA WORLD. When Baby Shamu was a young whale, he was a copycat calf. Wherever his mother went, he went. Whatever she did, he did. This type of behavior is called "mimicry," because what he saw is what he did. Many young animals are great mimics and learn their behavior from imitating others.

follow the leader

Me and my shadow. Whatever the mother whale does, the calf does, too.

Even adult whales learn faster when paired with experienced partners. Following the leader is a natural activity— and a big help to trainers.

In observational learning, a whale that mimics others is "observing" and "learning."

Shamu gets a pat for a job well done.

D◎ it again, SHAMU

The main way whales learn at SEA WORLD is through "operant conditioning." That may sound complicated, but it's simple to Shamu. Here's how it works.

Shamu is taught that when he hears a whistle blow, he did something good for which he will receive a reward. The reward is always something that Shamu enjoys, like a back scratch, a rubdown, or a fish. Shamu doesn't know what he will receive, he just knows it's something he likes. This keeps Shamu interested in learning new things.

REINFORCERS

People respond to reinforcers, too. Here's an example. You wave to someone. They wave back and greet you. That's your reinforcer. The two go together. If you waved and no one waved back, you'd stop waving.

Through "operant conditioning" Shamu learns to slide out of the water and wait for a trainer's signal (above left) or land from a jump with a big splash (above right).

Whales are playful, and really do have fun with their trainers.

Positive RESULTS

How do Shamu's trainers get him to repeat and improve a behavior? They can't say, "Great move, Shamu." Whales are smart, but English is not their language. Instead, they work through a system of "positive reinforcers," rewards that will encourage the whale to repeat a behavior.

Trainers choose positive reinforcers they *think* Shamu will like. But how's a trainer to know? Simple. If the reinforcer doesn't appeal to Shamu, he won't repeat the behavior as often.

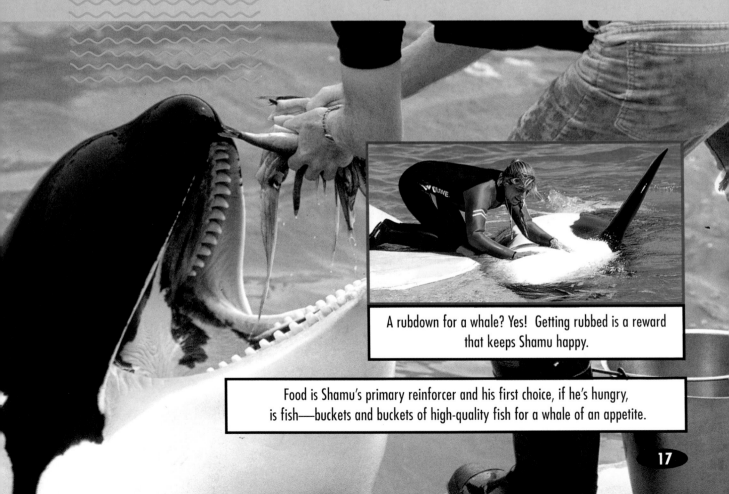

A rubdown for a whale? Yes! Getting rubbed is a reward that keeps Shamu happy.

Food is Shamu's primary reinforcer and his first choice, if he's hungry, is fish—buckets and buckets of high-quality fish for a whale of an appetite.

After Shamu has finished splashing the crowd, he will look for a bridge signal or a reinforcer

whistling
while they work

If Shamu is out in the middle of the pool and is too far away to get an immediate reward, the trainer sends him a "bridge signal," which can be a whistle. Then Shamu knows that a reinforcer is on the way.

An electronic tonal system is yet another helpful tool used in training.

SWACS

SWACS, the SEA WORLD Auditory Cueing System, is a new way to communicate with marine mammals. In this case the tones are based on calls of killer whales. They're created by computer codes. At SEA WORLD, even whales are affected by computers.

The target pole is really an extension of the trainer's hand. It reaches where she can't.

Tricky
LEARNING

It's fantastic to see Shamu do a rocket hop. He spikes straight out of the water—guiding his trainer standing on his nose! That's a complex behavior to learn, but Shamu makes it look easy. How does he do it? With a target. His trainer takes him through the motions, step-by-step, using a stick with a float on the end. Every time Shamu touches the stick, the trainer blows the whistle (conditioned reinforcer) and gives him a reward (positive reinforcer). It takes a lot of little steps (and rewards) to teach Shamu a behavior that makes a big splash.

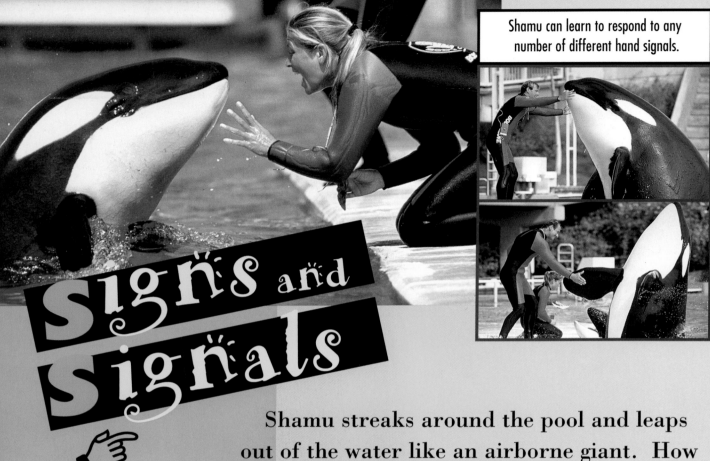

Shamu can learn to respond to any number of different hand signals.

Signs and Signals

Shamu streaks around the pool and leaps out of the water like an airborne giant. How does he know when to do that? He gets a signal. From outer space? No, from his trainers. When teaching Shamu, his trainers use signals along with a target. Then, when they take away the target, Shamu "knows" the signal.

Shamu will also recognize a tactile and/or an auditory signal.

TACTILE

VISUAL

AUDITORY

Signals can be "tactile," a touch; or "visual," a gesture; or "auditory," a voice command.

Imagine an 8,000-pound killer whale holding still to have his measurements taken—it can happen at SEA WORLD. One of the benefits of training is that whales can be taught to help trainers take better care of them. The research Shamu allows veterinarians and scientists to do is important in caring for him as well as to help wild killer whales thrive for generations to come.

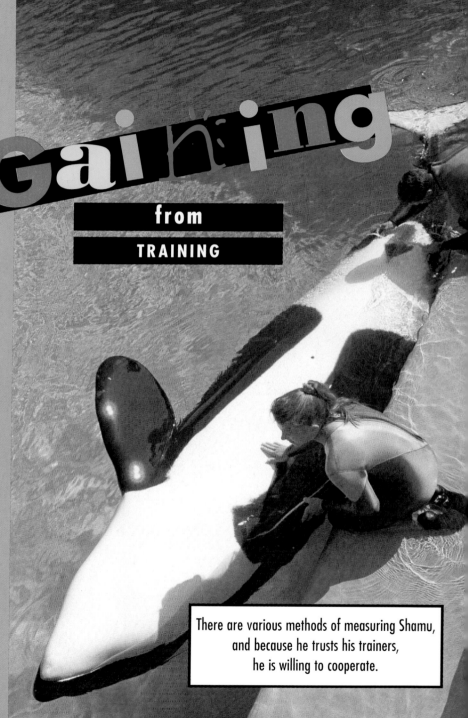

Gaining

from
TRAINING

There are various methods of measuring Shamu, and because he trusts his trainers, he is willing to cooperate.

Babies

Animal care specialists at SEA WORLD watch closely whenever a baby whale is present. They want to be sure that it is nursing properly. In the wild, 50% of first-year whales die, some possibly because they can't nurse.

A mother pygmy sperm whale and her month-old calf were rescued from a Florida beach and brought to SEA WORLD for nourishment and care.

Killer whales at SEA WORLD have been trained to float on their backs so that blood samples can be taken from their tail flukes, just as blood is drawn from our arms. These samples are then checked for infections, or even to learn if a whale is pregnant.

Save the WHALES

Five whales have blood samples taken at SEA WORLD.

Rescue

The research done at SEA WORLD has helped scientists in their efforts to rescue whales, an ongoing program that can be used all over the world.

Animal care specialists administer fluids to a rescued whale.

The huge habitat pool at SEA WORLD gives Shamu plenty of room to play.

With other whales or alone, Shamu has lots of room to flex his muscles.

Shamu's

SEA WORLD

Killer whales are big and they need big water. At SEA WORLD they've got it—six million gallons, and they use it all. The huge habitat pool is the place the public sees. Behind the scenes there are other areas for training, feeding and playing, including smaller pools that are used for smaller animals.

Killer whales eat about 3% of their body weight each day. That means an 8,000-pound whale is fed about 240 pounds of fish and squid every 24 hours. Chow time at SEA WORLD is a BIG event.

SEA WORLD "chefs" prepare another meal for Shamu.

fascinating FACTS

HEAVY DUTY

Here are the facts about the jumbo size of killer whales.
Males average 22 to 27 feet long and weigh between 8,000 and 12,000 pounds. The huskiest may weigh over 15,000 pounds.

WHAT'S A BLACK-AND-WHITE FLASH?

A killer whale zipping by at 22 miles per hour.
There's hardly a marine mammal in the ocean that can keep up.

LITTLE THINGS MEAN A LOT

The smallest a killer whale can be is seven to eight feet long and 300 pounds—
the size of a newborn. Only about half the calves born at sea survive.

IN YOUR FACE

A killer whale has:
Eyes about the same size as a cow's.
No sense of smell.
Ears that receive sound through the lower jawbone.
No manners. It swallows food without chewing.

CONGRATULATIONS, GRANDMA!

In 1985, the first killer whale was born at SEA WORLD in Florida. In 1993, that whale had a calf—the first second generation birth in a zoological environment.

SAY WHAT?

Killer whales make noises or communicate with each other in "clicks" and "whistles" and sounds that resemble moans, grunts, squeaks and creaking doors.

WHAT A LIFE

Killer whales have an estimated maximum life span of at least 35 years.

Glossary

BREACHING. A whale of a jump—clear out of the water.

CONDITIONED REINFORCER. A signal like a whistle that becomes a reinforcer when paired with a known positive reinforcer like food.

HULA. A learned behavior. Shamu stands half way out of the water and twirls.

LOBTAILING. Whack! A big splash with a whale's tail.

MIMICRY. The way animals learn by watching others.

POD. A pod is a group of whales.

POSITIVE REINFORCER. In training, when Shamu performs a behavior, he is given something that encourages him to repeat it. That reward, food for example, is called a positive reinforcer.

SPYHOPPING. A whale lifting half his body straight out of the water to look around.

SWAC. Sea World Auditory Cueing System. Tones that Shamu learns are sent under the water. The tones are used to direct behavior. They are auditory signals.

Sea World®

"For in the end we will conserve only what we love.
We will love only what we understand.
And we will understand only what we are taught."

Baba Dioum — noted Central African Naturalist

Since the first Sea World opened in 1964, more than 160 million people have experienced first-hand the majesty and mystery of marine life. Sea World parks have been leaders in building public understanding and appreciation for killer whales, dolphins, and a vast variety of other sea creatures.

Through its work in animal rescue and rehabilitation, breeding, animal care, research and education, Sea World demonstrates a strong commitment to the preservation of marine life and the environment.

Sea World provides all its animals with the highest-quality care including state-of-the-art facilities and stimulating positive reinforcement training programs. Each park employs full-time veterinarians, trainers, biologists and other animal care experts to provide 24-hour care. Through close relationships with these animals — relationships that are built on trust — Sea World's animal care experts are able to monitor their health every day to ensure their well-being. In short, all animals residing at Sea World are treated with respect, love and care.

If you would like more information about Sea World books, please write to us. We'd like to hear from you.

THIRD STORY BOOKS
955 Connecticut Avenue, Suite 1302
Bridgeport, CT 06607